Puss in Boots

Retold by
LINCOLN KIRSTEIN

Based on the story by
CHARLES PERRAULT

Illustrated by
ALAIN VAËS

Little, Brown and Company
Boston Toronto London

ALSO ILLUSTRATED BY ALAIN VAËS

The Wild Hamster
The Steadfast Tin Soldier
The Porcelain Pepper Pot

Library of Congress Cataloging-in-Publication Data

Kirstein, Lincoln, 1907–
    Puss in Boots/retold by Lincoln Kirstein ; illustrated by Alain Vaës.
    p.   cm.
    Summary: A retelling of the French fairy tale in which a clever cat
wins his master a fortune and the hand of a princess.
    ISBN 0-316-89506-7 (hc)
    ISBN 0-316-89501-6 (pb)
    [1. Fairy tales. 2. Folklore — France.] I. Vaës, Alain, ill. II. Title.
PZ8.K6194Pu 1992
398.24′52974428′0944 — dc20   91-19352

10 9 8 7 6 5 4

Published simultaneously in Canada
by Little, Brown & Company (Canada) Limited

Manufactured in China
Calligraphy by Colleen

A miller who had three sons was growing old and ill, sad and forgetful—when he paid for his flour, he'd drop coins and lose them. His two older sons were worried about his failing memory and forced him to write a will. The oldest was left the mill, the second, a donkey that took

flour to market, but to Robin, the youngest, a shy, bullied boy, was left only Puss, whose wretched job was to keep rats from the stored grain. Teasing Robin, his two brothers handed him a knife, advising him to skin Puss for his fur coat.

Puss had quietly saved a silver ecu he'd seen the old miller drop, and he told Robin to buy him a pair of boots. The shoe shop had a large stock of slippers, sandals, clogs, and boots. The cobbler suggested Puss purchase something with gold or silver buckles. But Puss chose stout cowhide boots, strong enough for muddy roads, marshy ground, or thick woods.

Outside the shoe shop, Robin began to realize how clever his Puss was. Puss's new boots were splendid. But now this cat demanded a strong linen bag with long strings. Robin was puzzled by Puss's plan. But he agreed to the bag, for the cat seemed his loyal companion, and as a lonely boy, he had no other.

Puss was a clever hunter. A hideous ogre had long terrified the kingdom, devouring everything in sight and frightening away the wild animals. Yet Puss found some carrots and young lettuce in a forgotten glade with which

to bait his bag. Hiding at the forest near the ogre's tower, Puss pulled the bag's cord at just the right moment and caught a pair of plump bunnies as a gift for the king.

At the palace gate, Puss was stopped by the guard. The cat explained he'd come with a gift of game for the king from his famous owner, the marquis of Carabas. The guard had never heard of the marquis, but Puss purred with such power that the guard dropped his weapon, permitting Puss to pass.

In the throne room, Puss bowed low before the king. The courtiers were
amazed to see so polite a cat. With an elegant gesture, Puss plucked the
pair of rabbits from his bag. "Your Majesty, please accept these from my

lord and master, the marquis of Carabas." Surprised, delighted, the king
sent this treat to his cook.

Puss rejoined Robin on the highway. He ordered the boy, "Off with your shirt and shorts. Jump in that pond. Now!" Robin was slow to obey. Puss mewed, "Ah! Still you don't trust me?" So Robin undressed, and Puss hid

his clothes behind a rock. The royal coach passed there every noon. When it rolled up, the cat started howling, "Help! Help! The marquis of Carabas, my master, is drowning. Help! Save him!"

The coach stopped. The king remembered the name of a marquis of Carabas who'd sent him rabbits. The king's pretty daughter leaned out to look, and thought Robin looked much braver and better than a mere marquis. The king commanded that new clothes be brought for Robin. Thus cat and grateful boy, much smarter now, resumed their journey.

On the king's highway, Robin and Puss met some peasants whose fields had been ravaged by the roaming ogre. They were starving. Puss promised that he would conquer the monster, and he gave them these instructions: "When the king's coach drives by, tell him that all these lands belong

to the marquis of Carabas." The hungry peasants agreed, hoping Puss would keep his promise to help them. The king indeed passed by that very afternoon and was impressed to hear that so much land was owned by a single lord.

Puss approached the ogre's tower. At its tip-top, the filthy ogre was burping and snorting over his disgusting dinner. In his turban was a magic feather, stolen from a ruined prince. The greedy, dirty giant had kept the whole kingdom famished because of his appetite, but he had not yet tasted raw cat. Brave and shrewd, Puss flattered the ogre for his famed

magic powers, although these, too, like the feather in his turban, were stolen property. "I've been told," purred Puss, "that Your Highness can do anything!"

"It's true," belched the ogre. "Ask me!"

"Ogre! Be a lion!" Puss yelled his command. A huge, angry lion, with cruel claws and terrible teeth, appeared and roared so loud that the cat's fur stood up straight, his tail a ramrod.

But Puss managed to meow, "Ogre! Be a mouse!" In a flash, the lion vanished, and a tiny mouse scampered across the filthy floor. Puss pounced. When he had finished, all that remained of the ogre was his turban and the magic feather.

Robin had been waiting for Puss at the door to the ogre's tower. Puss had sliced the feather from the turban—a drop of magic still remained. Passing the thin, hungry peasants on the road back, he made a wish: "May these fields be green again." Corn, grass, and wheat sprouted at once, just as though this were a dream.

At the palace, the king and his daughter welcomed the triumphant pair. Robin shyly accepted the courtiers' cheers, knowing that not he, but his cat, had beaten the ogre. In the midst of a magnificent wedding, the king gave Robin his bride. Everyone feasted on wedding cake baked from

freshly sprouted wheat. Puss became prime minister, and the feather's last flicker of magic turned his leather boots to pure soft gold. Every morning, seven mice brushed and polished them.